THE CROW'S TALE

A Lenni Lenape Native American Legend

Naomi Howarth

Frances Lincoln
Children's Books

In the dark depths of winter, far far away,
snow started falling at the cold break of day.

In a freezing thick blanket it covered the land,
and the animals knew that they needed a plan.
They were tired and famished and frozen from cold –
until Wise Owl came up with a plan brave and bold.

"A perilous journey will need to be done.
Our bravest and best must go to the Sun.
Without the Sun's warmth we'll have nothing to eat.
So – which one of you will ask for some heat?"

ALL of the animals wanted to go,
but no one could do it except...

... Rainbow Crow!

With his radiant feathers and sweet singing voice,
the animals knew they had made the right choice.
The magnificently coloured kaleidoscope Crow
was the one who would battle through ice, wind and snow.

Up through the storm brave Crow quickly flew,
though the snow blurred his vision and the wind –
    how it blew!
Closer and closer he came to the Sun,
but his troubles and trials had only begun.

Crow flew through the blizzard, then to his delight
he entered Sun's kingdom of dazzling bright light.

"Oh, please, Mr Sun, we beg you to help,
to stop the snow falling. Oh, please make it melt!"
But wizened old Sun was in such a deep slumber,
he opened his eyes and roared loud as thunder –

"What IS all this racket? I've no time for whining.
I'm tired, I have just spent a whole summer shining.
What I will give you is a long branch of fire,
which will help keep you animals warmer and drier."

Thanking the Sun, and grasping the light,
Crow turned around for the long homeward flight.
Through terrible storms he tossed and tumbled
while the heavens shook and the skies loudly rumbled.
Holding the bright, burning branch with his foot,
Crow's colourful feathers got covered in soot.

Sooty and croaky,

scorched, singed and blackened,

Crow was unrecognisable from his beak to his backend.

Courageous, undaunted, he pressed on alone,
and all of the animals welcomed him home.

They marvelled and wondered, surprised and amazed
at the power and the strength of the fire as it blazed.
But seeing his feathers, Crow started to weep,
and bright droplets of tears slid down his beak.

Waking from slumber high up in the sky,
the all-seeing Sun saw Crow bitterly cry.
"What's wrong, my dear friend? Oh, what can it be?
You've shown kindness and keenness and such bravery."

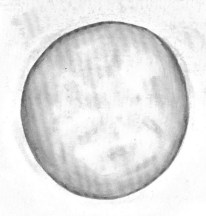

"The animals loved me for my colourful wings,
and now I can croak but once I could sing!
My feathers," said Crow, "are as burnt as can be.
Now none of the others will ever like me!"

"Dear Crow," said the Sun,
"you are selfless and brave.
It's not how you look, but how you behave.
Can you not see what the others can see?
You're as beautiful as you can possibly be."

Crow looked at his feathers. It was then that he knew,
from the deep shades of violet and bright hues of blue,
that his glossy new self was a gift from the Sun
to honour and treasure the deed he had done.

Pretty or ugly, slim, thin or fatter,
your beauty inside is the heart of the matter.